for

EMMA CLARE BURROWS

TRENTON, NEW JERSEY

at age three months

23 MAY 1988

from GRANDPA and GRANDMA BURROWS

in KATOOMBA, BLUE MOUNTAINS,

NEW SOUTH WALES

100 MILES WEST OF SYDNEY,

AUSTRALIA

with love and kisses !

Shortly before she died in 1969, May Gibbs gave approval for her work to be adapted for the Young Australia Series. It was her wish that her original characters should be faithfully reproduced, as they have been by Noela Young in her sensitive illustrations.

Humans! Please be kind to all Bush Creatures and don't pull flowers up by the roots.

ANGUS & ROBERTSON PUBLISHERS

Unit 4, Eden Park, 31 Waterloo Road,
North Ryde, NSW, Australia 2113, and
16 Golden Square, London W1R 4BN,
United Kingdom

This adaptation first published in Australia
by Angus & Robertson Publishers in 1975
Reprinted 1984, 1985, 1986, 1987

ISBN 0 207 13264 X

Printed in Singapore

Snugglepot and Cuddlepie

ON BOARD THE SNAG

The original characters created by

MAY GIBBS

Redrawn by Noela Young

Adapted by David Harris

ANGUS & ROBERTSON PUBLISHERS

The bad Banksia men were angry with Snugglepot and Cuddlepie and Ragged Blossom. This was because Mrs Snake, who was the friend of the bad Banksia men, had been killed by Mr Lizard and of course Mr Lizard was the friend of Snugglepot and Cuddlepie and Ragged Blossom too.

"We must get rid of those stupid Nuts," they said, "and then their friend Mr Lizard will be so sad that he might die too and then we will be rid of our greatest enemy."

"Smoke and burn him," growled a bad Banksia man.

"Drop and drown him," snarled another.

"Ha," said the biggest Banksia man, "that's a good idea. We'll drown them. Ha! Ha! Listen."

Then all the bad Banksia men put their heads together and began to work out a wicked plan.

Now it happened that a friend of Mr Lizard was sitting among the bushes right under the tree where the Banksia men were talking together. When he heard them mention Mr Lizard's name he listened carefully to what the Banksia men were saying. When he heard their awful plan to drown the Nuts, he crept softly away till he was out of sight then dashed along as fast as he could to find Mr Lizard and tell him what he had heard.

But sad to say he wasn't able to tell Mr Lizard the news. For Mr Lizard had had far too much to eat last night at Mr Pilly's party and he had to stay in bed all day. His head was aching and the flies were worrying him and he was so cross that no one could go near him. When his friend came running along to tell him the news Mr Lizard yelled, "Go away! I'm sick! Go away!" And he lashed his tail and wouldn't listen to a word, so his friend had to go away and couldn't tell him the news.

While Mr Lizard was lying in his bed, a big ship was lying in the harbour. The Captain had come ashore, and had invited Ragged Blossom and Snugglepot and Cuddlepie to go on a long journey with him to visit new countries.

Many of the other Nuts and Blossoms said they would like to go too, and so it was decided that the ship, which was named *The Snag,* should sail at once. So everybody was busy packing.

In their excitement Snugglepot and Cuddlepie forgot all about Mr Lizard but as the ship was moving out into the stream, the noise of the crowd shouting on the wharf woke their friend. He sprang out of bed and rushed wildly down to the water calling, "Stop! Stop! Wait for me!"

Everyone on the wharf began to join in yelling, "Stop, stop!"

Snugglepot and Cuddlepie saw Mr Lizard and ran to the Captain, begging him to go back to the wharf. But the Captain, who was a big stern man with a great beard and bushy eyebrows, frowned at them and said, "The tide's going out and we must go with it."

Then Snugglepot and Cuddlepie were very sad, and Ragged Blossom dropped tears into the sea as she hung over the side waving to poor Mr Lizard.

"Oh, why did we forget him?" moaned Snugglepot.

"He was so kind to me," wailed Ragged Blossom.

"Our dear old friend," sobbed Cuddlepie.

Mr Lizard was so upset at being left behind that he jumped into a little boat and rowed after them. He rowed as hard as he could, and the Nuts shouted, "Come on!" as the little boat got nearer and nearer to the big ship. But alas! just as he was nearly touching the side, the breeze caught the big green sails and away went *The Snag* to sea, leaving Mr Lizard and his little boat far behind, like a speck in the distance. Mr Lizard sat very still in his boat, staring after *The Snag*. He was very angry and very sad.

"Oh, Gum! Gum! Gum!" he groaned. Then he fell in a heap in the bottom of the boat filled with grief and anger for he had seen the Captain and he knew who he was!

You see the big Captain with his thick beard and bushy eyebrows was none other than the biggest and baddest of the Banksia men. "And no one on board will guess that," cried Mr Lizard.

The air was fresh and the little waves danced and sparkled in the sun as *The Snag* sailed gracefully on, very like a big green butterfly on a blue sea. Everybody walked up and down the deck laughing and chatting. Snugglepot and Cuddlepie and Ragged Blossom walked up and down too and it was all so exciting and lovely that they very soon forgot poor Mr Lizard. They were having so much fun that they didn't notice that the waves were growing bigger all the time, and the wind was becoming stronger.

"Isn't it gummy!" said Ragged Blossom.

"Treetop!" cried Cuddlepie.

"Juicy!" chuckled Snugglepot.

And all the time the waves were getting bigger and bigger.

"Look at all those people leaning over the side. I wonder what they're looking at?" said Cuddlepie.

"Oh!" said Snugglepot. "I feel strange!"

"So do I," said Ragged Blossom.

"I've got a pain in my tummy," groaned Cuddlepie.

"I feel stranger and stranger," said Snugglepot.

"I think I'd like to go to bed," said Ragged Blossom.

Just then *The Snag* rose up over a huge wave and they all sat down and slid along the deck. Then *The Snag* rose up at the other end and they all slid back again.

"I don't like it," said Ragged Blossom.

"I hate it," said Snugglepot.

"So do I," said Cuddlepie.

The boat rocked from side to side and the Nuts slid up and down the deck. Then as they were sliding along the deck one more time they suddenly felt themselves falling down a dark hole into the bottom of the ship. They landed on a big pile of feathers.

"Where are we?" said Cuddlepie.

"In the bottom of the boat, I think," said Snugglepot.

"Hush," whispered Ragged Blossom. "I can hear voices."

They all kept very still and listened; and some way off in the darkness they heard the Captain's voice. "Now listen very carefully," he was saying. "As soon as the moon is gone and everything is dark, over the side they go — all three of them — do you follow?"

"Ay, Ay! Sir," said a gruff voice.

"You do your work quickly," said the Captain, "and I'll see you get paid well. And not a word to anyone. Understand?"

"Ay, Ay! Sir," said the gruff voice.

The Nuts were terrified. They now realized who the Captain was and they knew he meant them to be thrown into the sea as soon as it was dark. They heard the Captain and the sailor climb up the ladder out of the ship's hold, and walk away.

"It's the Banksia man," whispered Snugglepot.

"What shall we do?" asked Ragged Blossom.

"The moon is shining now," said Snugglepot, "so we are safe for a little while."

"Let's hide in one of those big empty nuts," said Cuddlepie.

"Oh that's a good idea," said Snugglepot, "and I'll go and find some food."

"Do be careful no one sees you," said Ragged Blossom.

"I'll be cunning as a dingo," said Snugglepot, and off he went up the long ladder, for he was very brave.

By this time Cuddlepie and Ragged Blossom had grown used to the dark hold and could see the things that were lying around them. There were passengers' trunks and bags, and a stack of huge nuts. As they crept about, they heard a noise behind some bundles of clothes-props.

"What was that?" whispered Ragged Blossom.

"I don't know. I'll go and see," said Cuddlepie.

"Oh! Look! Look!" exclaimed Ragged Blossom. And there quite close to them, poking out of a crack, was the end of a grey tail. Cuddlepie grabbed it and pulled, but the owner of the tail held fast.

"Come out," cried Cuddlepie, "or I'll pull your tail off."

"Oh! Oh!" squeaked a little voice. "Let me go, and I'll come out."

"Very well, quick-sticks," said Cuddlepie, and out crept a thin pale little rat, with big frightened eyes and nervous whiskers.

"What's your name?" asked Cuddlepie.

"Jerboa," said the poor little chap. "But most people call me Winky."

"Are you a stowaway?" asked Cuddlepie.

"Yes, Sir," answered Winky.

"Where are you going?" asked Cuddlepie.

"Back to my mother, please Sir," said the poor little fellow, with tears in his eyes. "I ran away from home to look for raisins, and I lost myself, I did, and I had an unhappy time. Snakes nearly ate me, and owls nearly ate me, and the Banksia men beat me; and I hid aboard this ship, when I heard them say it was bound for Big Bad City, and I want to go home to my mother, I do; and I'm so hungry and cold. Sir, please don't tell the Captain."

"Poor little man," said Ragged Blossom. "We'll give you some food when Snugglepot comes."

Cuddlepie sat down with Winky and told him all about how the bad Captain wanted to drown them. "So, you see, we must hide down here too, and we'll all help each other."

"Well," said little Winky eagerly, "we shall get to Big Bad City tonight, and I can show you a way off the ship."

"Oh, can you?" said Cuddlepie and Ragged Blossom. "How kind of you!"

All at once Snugglepot came rushing down the ladder as fast as he could. "We're nearly into a city and" — then seeing Winky he stopped in amazement.

"He's our friend," said Cuddlepie, and he told Snugglepot what had happened. When Snugglepot had heard the story he took out all the food he had brought back and there was enough for everyone. As they finished their meal they realized that the ship was pulling into a wharf and tying up.

Snugglepot and Cuddlepie and Ragged Blossom followed Winky up out of the hold and along the deck in the shadow of the side. As they were creeping along, a funny old woman, who was running about looking for her luggage, tripped on the end of Winky's long tail. She screamed loudly and the Nuts and Winky stood very still, terrified that they might be discovered, but there was so much noise and bustle that no one took any notice, and so they crept up along the deck until they came to a place where a big rope was tied from the ship's side across to the wharf.

"Now," said Winky, "this is the way. Cling to me and I'll take you over one at a time."

When they were safely landed on the wharf, Winky said, "Follow me as fast as you can." He ran off into a dark shed, and they all ran after him.

It was a long run — over fences, down roads, across bridges, through gardens, over roofs till at last everyone was tired out and it was getting light and all the birds were chirping to each other.

So they sat down by the side of the road to rest for a little while. They looked about them and discovered that they were sitting at the side of a broad road with large houses on each side. Gradually the sun rose and they sat warming themselves and feeling a little less tired.

"It's only a little way to my home now," said Winky, and he led them down a lane to a dear little house all made of branches. Poor Winky. On the door was a note to say that everyone was away looking for him. He began to cry.

"Never mind," said Ragged Blossom. "I'm sure they won't be away for very long."

Winky cheered up a little and showed them over his home. "I'd like you to stay with me," he said, "till you get a home of your own."

"Thank you, dear Winky," they said. "We'd love to do that."

"Well now," said Winky. "Let's have something to eat and then I'll show you around Big Bad City."

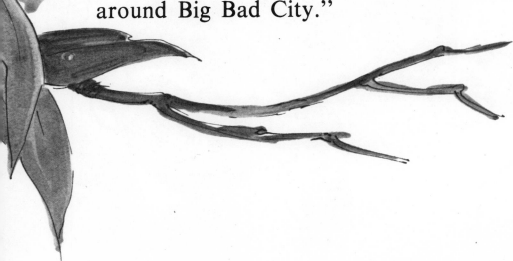

After their meal Winky took the Nuts out into the busy streets of Big Bad City. Snugglepot and Cuddlepie and Ragged Blossom looked about them in amazement. There was so much to see. People were hurrying in and out of shops and standing about on the sides of the streets talking to each other. They wore such beautiful clothes, and some of the Gumnut ladies were carrying beautiful umbrellas. Out on the road, cars were rushing backwards and forwards and young Nuts were racing by on scooters. All the rush and noise made the Nuts feel quite nervous.

As they walked along past all the shops they came to a large paddock where a big crowd of Nuts were watching a football match. Snugglepot and Cuddlepie and Ragged Blossom had never seen such a game before but it was very exciting and they joined in the cheering as the Nuts on the field ran up and down chasing each other. Every now and then they all fell in a big heap which Winky told them was called a scrum. When the game was over they were feeling very tired and decided it was time to go home to Winky's place.

"Tomorrow we must go out and look for a job," said Snugglepot.

"Yes," said Cuddlepie. "I wonder what kind of work we will find to do in Big Bad City."

As they wandered wearily home to Winky's snug little house they had forgotten all about the bad Banksia men and their wicked plans. They had also forgotten about their dear friend Mr Lizard, but poor Mr Lizard had not forgotten about them, and neither had the bad Banksia men.